THE MAGIC DREIDELS

This **PJ BOOK** belongs to

_____

_____

PJ Library®

JEWISH BEDTIME STORIES and SONGS

To Rose and Mayer Zar
E.A.K.

For my parents, Alla and Anatoli, with love
K.K.

THE MAGIC DREIDELS

A Hanukkah Story

Eric A. Kimmel

illustrated by Katya Krenina

Holiday House/New York

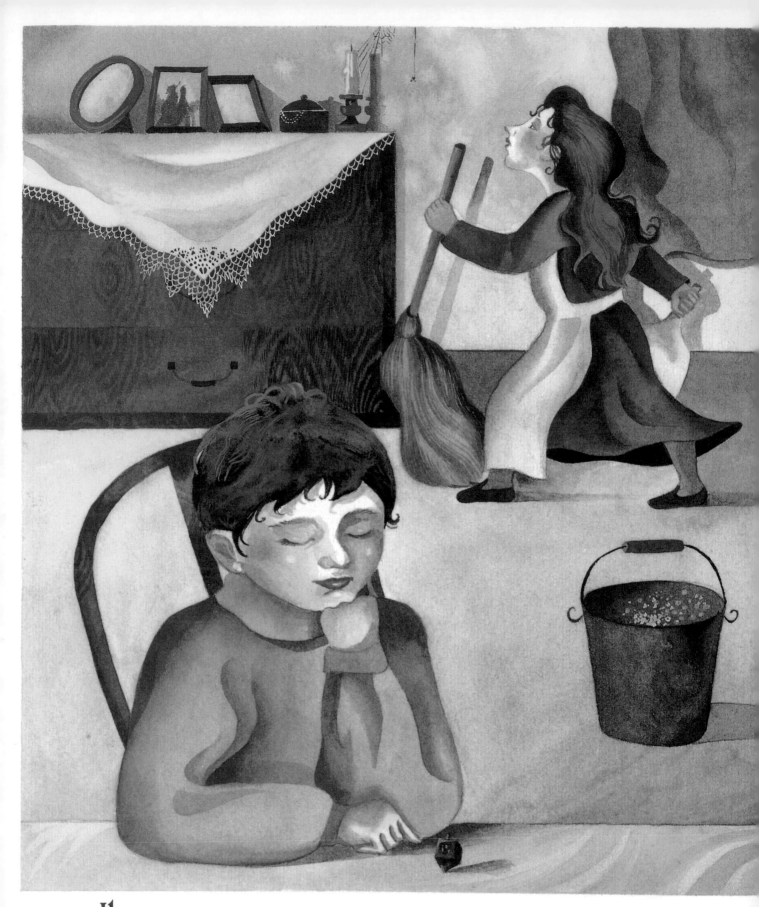

Hanukkah was coming. Everyone in Jacob's family worked hard, cleaning and scrubbing, polishing and sweeping to get ready.

That is, everyone except Jacob. Jacob sat playing with his new brass dreidel.

When his mother sent him to the well to fetch a bucket of water, Jacob took the dreidel with him.

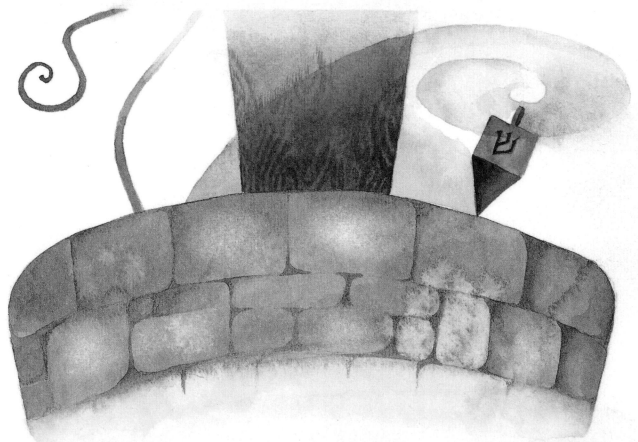

After filling the bucket, Jacob decided to give the dreidel a spin. The dreidel spun across the mossy stones and plopped in the well.

"My dreidel! I've lost my new brass dreidel," Jacob cried. "Maybe I can get it back again. Maybe I can splash it out." He started dropping rocks into the water.

Now, a goblin lived at the bottom of the well. He was a peace-
ful goblin who never bothered anyone. Suddenly rocks began
falling on his head.

The goblin rushed to the surface. "Who's dropping rocks on me?" he shouted.

"I didn't mean to drop rocks on you. I just want my new brass dreidel back," Jacob replied.

"I'll find your dreidel," the goblin muttered.

He dove under the water. Soon he reappeared, carrying a wooden dreidel.

"I can't find your dreidel. Take this one. It's magic. It spins out latkes," the goblin said.

Jacob ran home to show everyone his magic dreidel.
Along the way he passed the house of Fruma Sarah, the neighborhood busybody. "Why are you running so fast, Jacob?" she asked.

"I have a new dreidel. It spins out latkes," Jacob told her. He spun the magic dreidel. Out came latkes, steaming hot, drenched with applesauce and sour cream.

"Oh! Look how muddy that dreidel is. Let me clean it for you." Fruma Sarah took the magic dreidel inside her house. She came back with an ordinary wooden dreidel.

Jacob took the ordinary dreidel home.

"Where have you been?" his mother asked. "And where is the bucket of water I sent you to bring?"

"This is more important than a bucket of water, Mother," Jacob explained. "I dropped my new brass dreidel in the well. A goblin who lives at the bottom gave me another one. It spins out latkes with applesauce and sour cream."

Jacob's mother refused to believe him.

"Watch, I'll show you," Jacob said. He spun the dreidel. Nothing happened.

"Just as I thought," said his mother. "Go back to the well and stop wasting my time with foolishness."

Jacob returned to the well. "Goblin!" he called. The goblin came rushing up. "What's the matter now?"

"Give back my brass dreidel. The wooden one you gave me is no good."

"I don't have your old dreidel, but I'll give you this one." The goblin gave Jacob a silver dreidel. "This dreidel is magic. It spins out Hanukkah gelt."

Jacob ran home with the silver dreidel.

He passed Fruma Sarah's house. "Hello, Jacob! Did you find another dreidel?" she asked.

"I did!" Jacob said. "This one spins out Hanukkah gelt. Watch!" Jacob spun the magic dreidel. Out came silver coins!

"Oh, but look how tarnished it is," Fruma Sarah said. "Let me polish it for you." She took the magic dreidel inside and exchanged it for an ordinary one.

Jacob took the ordinary dreidel and ran home.

"Look, everybody! This dreidel spins out Hanukkah gelt!" Jacob's family gathered around to see. He spun the dreidel again and again, but not even a penny came out.

"Jacob, this is no time for foolishness," his father said. "You should be ashamed of yourself. Can't you see how hard everyone is working, trying to get ready for Hanukkah? Yet here you are, spending your time playing tricks and getting in the way."

He sent Jacob to his room.

Poor Jacob! Nobody believed him. He had to prove he was telling the truth. When no one was looking, he climbed out the window and ran to the well.

"Goblin, come out!" he called.

The goblin came rushing up. "What do you want now, Jacob?"

"I want my good brass dreidel. The silver one you gave me didn't work either."

"The dreidels work," the goblin said. "Fruma Sarah stole them and gave you ordinary dreidels in their place."

"So that's what happened!" Jacob exclaimed. "Goblin, help me get my dreidels back, and I'll bother you no more."

The goblin dove to the bottom of the well. He came up a few minutes later, carrying an iron dreidel.

"Let Fruma Sarah spin this one. She will give back the ones she stole," the goblin said.

Jacob took the iron dreidel. On the way home he stopped at
Fruma Sarah's house.

"I have another dreidel," Jacob said.

"What does it do?" Fruma Sarah asked.

"Come try it!"

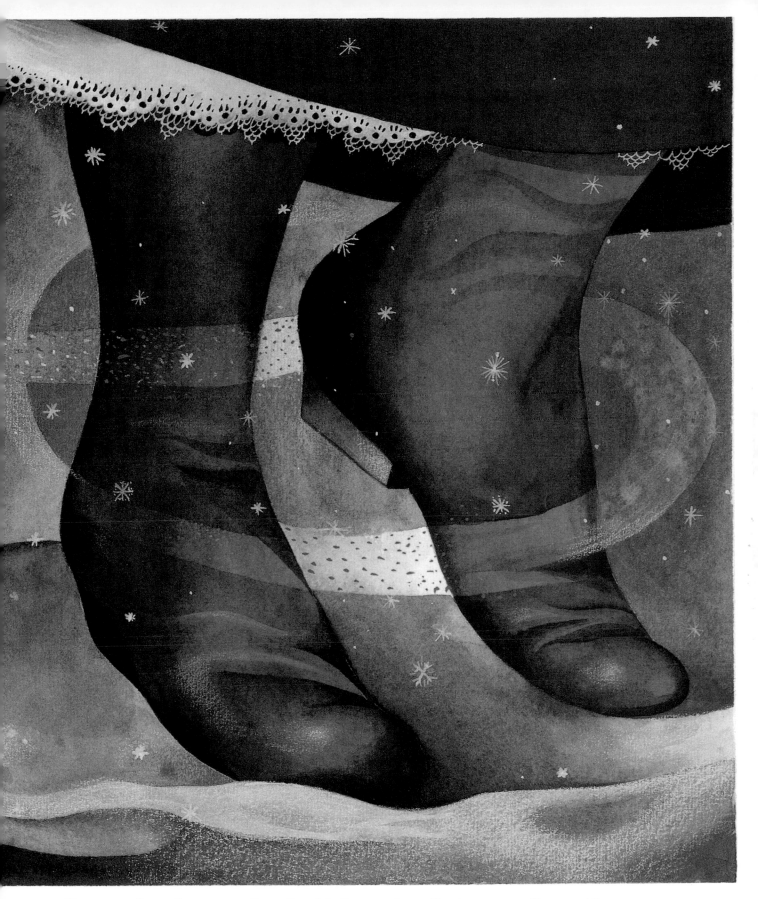

Fruma Sarah gave the dreidel a spin. Out came fleas, thousands of them! They hopped on Fruma Sarah and began to bite. Fruma Sarah scratched and itched. "Oh, oh, oh! I'll give back the dreidels I stole. Just make these fleas stop biting!"

Fruma Sarah returned the two dreidels she had hidden in her apron. Only then did the fleas hop away.

Jacob took the magic dreidels and ran to the well. He threw in the iron dreidel. "Thank you, Goblin, for helping me," he called. "I'll keep the first two you gave me. You can have this one. I don't need it anymore."

He turned around and ran all the way home.

Jacob didn't mention the magic dreidels until the Hanukkah candles were lit. Then he took them out and spun them one after another. The first dreidel spun out potato latkes.

Jacob and his family ate as much as they could hold.

The second spun out Hanukkah gelt.
They stuffed their pockets with silver coins and invited the
neighbors to share.

Everyone had a happy Hanukkah that night.

Even Fruma Sarah.

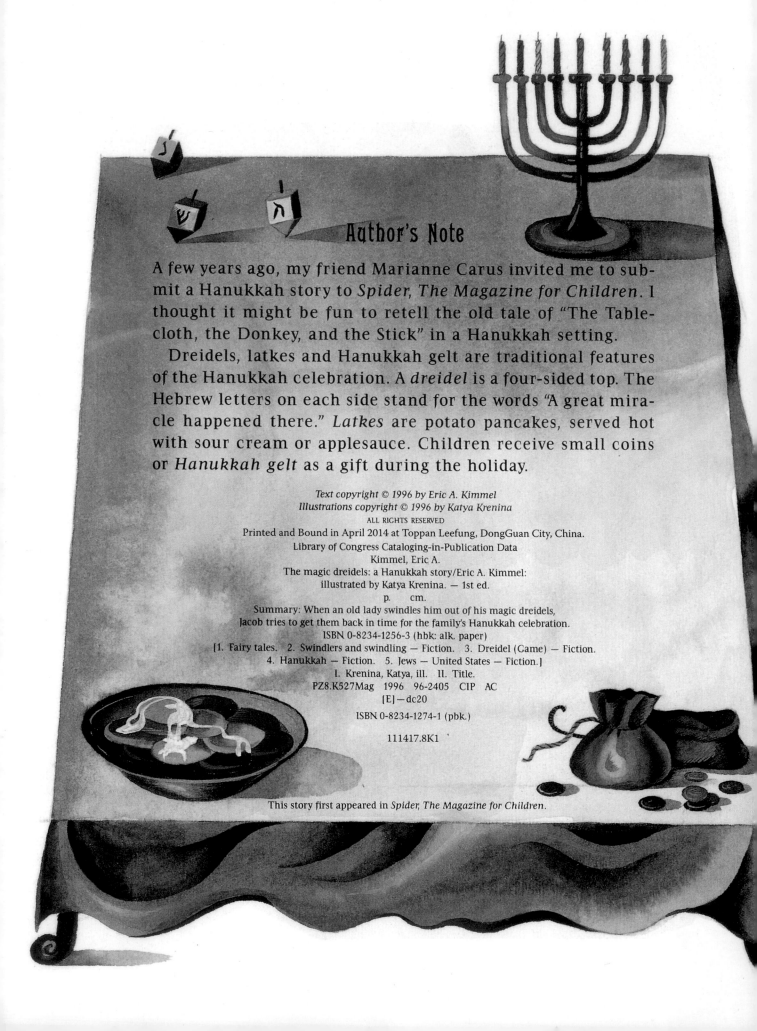

Author's Note

A few years ago, my friend Marianne Carus invited me to submit a Hanukkah story to *Spider, The Magazine for Children*. I thought it might be fun to retell the old tale of "The Tablecloth, the Donkey, and the Stick" in a Hanukkah setting.

Dreidels, latkes and Hanukkah gelt are traditional features of the Hanukkah celebration. A *dreidel* is a four-sided top. The Hebrew letters on each side stand for the words "A great miracle happened there." *Latkes* are potato pancakes, served hot with sour cream or applesauce. Children receive small coins or *Hanukkah gelt* as a gift during the holiday.

Text copyright © 1996 by Eric A. Kimmel
Illustrations copyright © 1996 by Katya Krenina
ALL RIGHTS RESERVED
Printed and Bound in April 2014 at Toppan Leefung, DongGuan City, China.
Library of Congress Cataloging-in-Publication Data
Kimmel, Eric A.
The magic dreidels: a Hanukkah story/Eric A. Kimmel:
illustrated by Katya Krenina. — 1st ed.
p.   cm.
Summary: When an old lady swindles him out of his magic dreidels,
Jacob tries to get them back in time for the family's Hanukkah celebration.
ISBN 0-8234-1256-3 (hbk: alk. paper)
[1. Fairy tales.   2. Swindlers and swindling — Fiction.   3. Dreidel (Game) — Fiction.
4. Hanukkah — Fiction.   5. Jews — United States — Fiction.]
I. Krenina, Katya, ill.   II. Title.
PZ8.K527Mag 1996   96-2405   CIP   AC
[E] — dc20

ISBN 0-8234-1274-1 (pbk.)

111417.8K1

This story first appeared in *Spider, The Magazine for Children*.